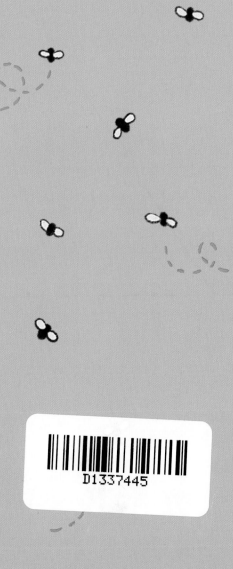

For Martin and Sue
~ HE

For my friends
~ JL

CATERPILLAR BOOKS
An imprint of the Little Tiger Group
www.littletiger.co.uk
1 Coda Studios, 189 Munster Road, London SW6 6AW
First published in Great Britain 2019
This edition published in 2020
Text by Harriet Evans
Text copyright © Caterpillar Books Ltd 2019
Illustrations copyright © Jacqui Lee 2019
A CIP Catalogue record for this book is available from the British Library
All rights reserved • Printed in China
ISBN: 978-1-84857-994-1 • CPB/1800/1373/0320
10 9 8 7 6 5 4 3 2 1

Harriet Evans

Jacqui Lee

This is
FROG

LiTTLE TiGER
LONDON

This is Frog.
Well, actually, this is Tree Frog,
but his friends call him Frog.
Frog lives in the rainforest.

Shall we help Frog jump by
shaking the book up and down?

Frog?

Oh dear...

Quick, let's follow him!
Use your fingers to run up
the page after Frog.

Wait, what are you
doing upside down, Frog?
You're making me dizzy!

Push Frog the right way up onto
the branch with your hand.

That's better.
Ooh, look – flies! Yum!

Can you blow them towards Frog?

Lots of tasty snacks.

og, you must know what to do now!

at, Frog? You've forgotten?
our tongue to remind Frog.

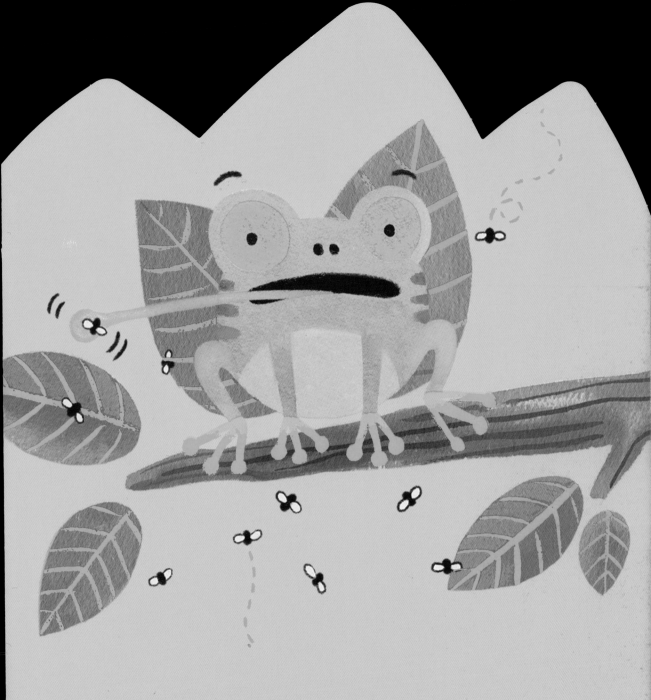

Well done. Give Frog a cheer!

Mmm, delicious.
The other flies are buzzing off!

Tap them as fast as you can to show
Frog where to find the rest of his meal.

All gobbled up now.
Hey, Frog, it looks as if
a friend has come to visit.

Tilt the page to help Frog move closer.

Uh-oh. Maybe not a friend!

Croak loudly as a warning.

Quick – pull the book
towards you to save Frog!

Phew! That was close.
Frog's still a bit scared.

Can you move this leaf over
him for camouflage?

And another, just in case?

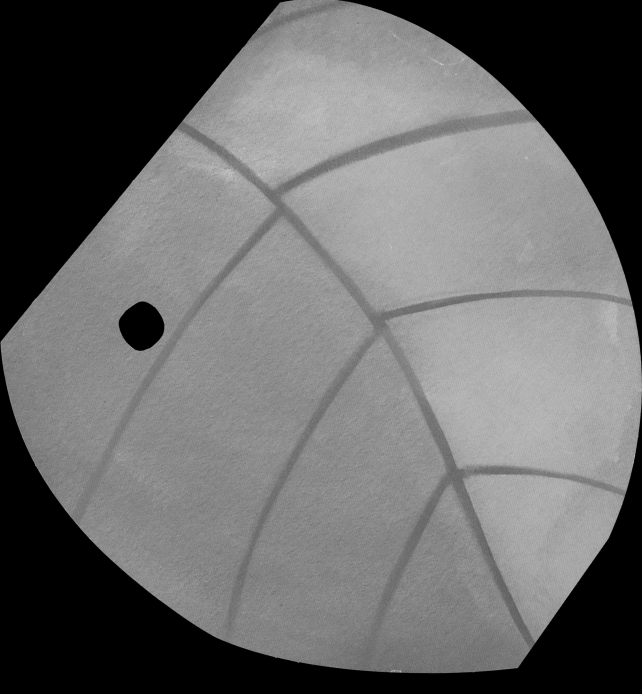

Hurray! But wait –
who else is hanging out
on Frog's branch?

Frog is not a big fan
of strangers.

Shake the book to
make them hop off.

Oops! Maybe you shook a bit too hard...

Spin the book all the way
around to help Frog land
the right way up.

Great work! Give yourself a round of applause.

Hang on – is it starting to rain?

Can you count the drops?

Oh no, the rain's getting heavier!

Move the flower over Frog to shelter him from the monsoon.

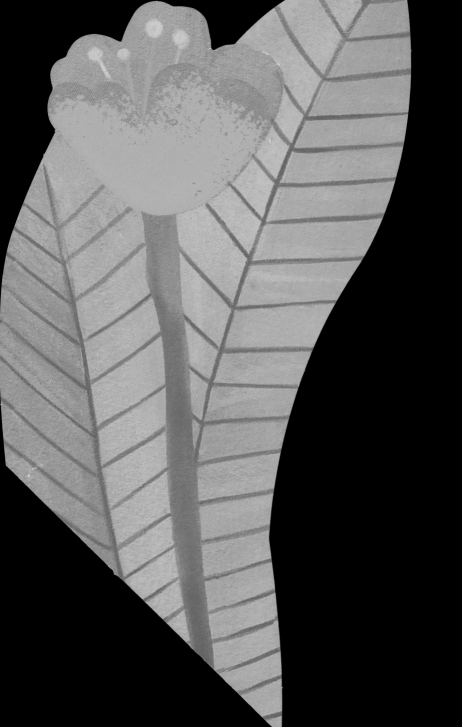

Oh, sorry, Frog,
I forgot you *like* water!
Let's help him jump
into the pool
below.

Turn the book sideways to prepare for Frog's jump.

Whoa, it's a long way down!

Can you trace a path with
your finger along the vines
for Frog to follow?

That's quite a big splash
for such a small frog.

Try brushing aside the water so that we can see Frog again.

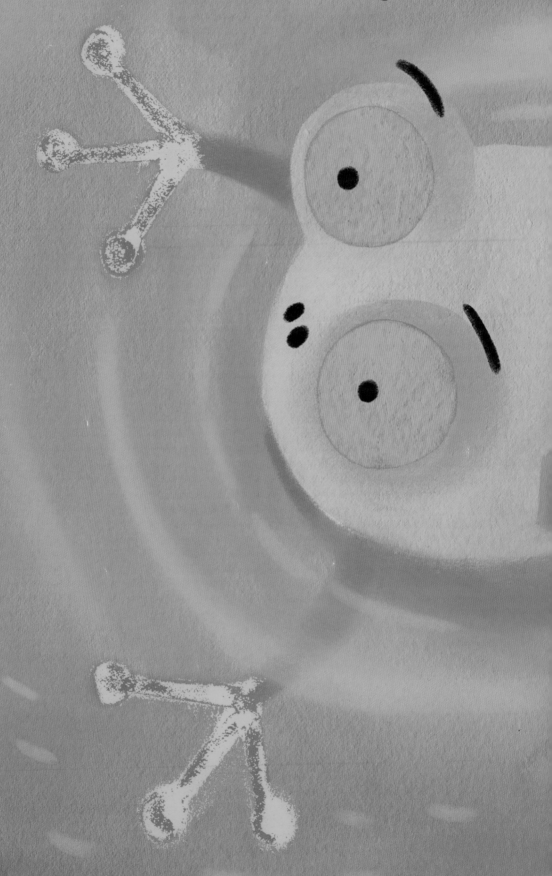

There you are, Frog!

Frog's jump has spun him all over the place. Can you turn the book back?

Flap the pages to help
him swim froggy-paddle.

Okay, that's enough of that.
Frog's a tree frog so he prefers
jumping to swimming.

Can you bounce the book on your knee
to help Frog jump onto the bank?

On dry land again – tree-rific!
Come on, Frog, let's hop back
onto your branch.

Frog?

Poor Frog looks tired out, it might be a
while before he can climb the tree...

Maybe you can help!

Shut the book and shake it to
revive Frog so that he's ready for
another un-frog-ettable adventure!